SPERO

Aanandi Sidharth

SPERO

Aanandi Sidharth

SPERO *by* Aanandi Sidharth

Copyright © Aanandi Sidharth, 2017

Aanandi Sidharth asserts the moral right to be identified as the author of this book. No reproduction without permission.

ALL RIGHTS RESERVED. No part of this book may be reproduced or transmitted in any form by any means, electronic or mechanical, including photocopying and recording, or by any information storage and retrieval system, except as may be expressly permitted in writing by the publisher.

Published in 2017 by www.pblishing.com

Marketed by

Maple Press Private Limited
Sales Office A 63, Sector 58, Noida 201 301, U.P., India
phone +91 120 455 3581, 455 3583
email info@**maple**press.co.in
website www.**maple**press.co.in

ISBN: 978-93-87348-04-2

10 9 8 7 6 5 4 3 2 1

This wouldn't have been possible without you.
Thank you for always being there,
Sakshi Chandak.

Acknowledgement

Throughout this whole process, there have been many people who have helped me reach the finish line.

I would like to thank Neeraj uncle for encouraging me to write this book and do something that I had always deemed as impossible. I would like to thank my **parents, my brothers and everyone in my family, for** providing me an unconditional support and reassurance throughout this endeavor.

I would also like to thank pblishing.com for making this dream into a reality.

CONTENTS

SYNOPSIS

Spero is an attempt made by a debut author to make people understand that they're not alone. As while, what one goes through may not exactly coincide with the other's predicament, the inner feelings and turmoil that we all go through, roots from the same reasons. We all have our insecurities, our fears, our doubts and by knowing that there are people like us going through the same as we, gives us solace.

In Latin, Spero means 'hope' and this book works to give people a hope to know that everything is going to be okay.

There are many incidents quoted in this book that are taken from the real-life scenarios. The aim of this book is to help people understand what they're going through and how they could help others as well as themselves in this process of growing up.

PROLOGUE

Millions of lives. A million faces. A million thoughts. And even more problems.

Throughout all this, there is one thing they all have in common- that we're all alone. Never realizing that we couldn't be further from the truth.

We may seem different, look different, walk differently, and talk differently. But at the end, the problems which we go through have originated from the same place, it just takes different forms.

So, no matter how much it feels like at times, **we're never alone. There is a hope.**

CHAPTER 1

PEOPLE

"No friendship is an accident."

-O. Henry

The people we meet throughout our lives have left their marks on us, whether we may realize this or not. The changes may lie in the little things we do - the things we like or something that may alter our entire existence. But, no matter how big or small the changes, who we are today, there have been influenced by everyone we have met throughout our existence.

They may be mere acquaintances, whom we met down the hall or they might be the people whom we have grown to spend every waking hour with. No matter what the relationship or the length of it may have been, we would have learnt something unforgettable in our lives through them.

Now, sometimes these friendships may only be fleeting, and seem to have started and finished at the blink of an eye. They may not seem significant or something we even remember as time passes, but even just getting a quick glimpse into what their world looks like, or witnessing an instance that they went through that resulted in them changing the tracks of their life has more significance than we think. The technicalities of what we have actually got from them doesn't matter, but the fact that we were able to make a connection with an another individual is what makes it valuable.

Something we all forget is how rare it is to make a pure connection to someone, like doing something that both of you are passionate about , having a heated debate on issues that are important to both of you or even talking to someone about what we did in our day. Most of the times, we are too used to just making friends or there are other things that plague our mind which makes us forget to value this simple connection.

While there may be various short friendships which we have had in our lives, there will be another bigger or smaller range of people whom we have deemed close enough to us to share our deepest, darkest secrets with. These are the ones that influence us the most and they are the people that we have learnt the most from. Even in these groups, there are people we may be closer to, or people we have known for longer or just some people whom we find to vibrating at the same frequency as us. As we get to know them better, there is an insight that we get into their world, that opens us into this extremely different world than what we may be used to.

There are times when I feel it isn't possible for me to make long-lasting friendships with people like the way the rest of the people I know do. People around me had friendships that started when they couldn't even speak and have remained together ever since. Or I just felt that their friendships were just better than the bonds that I seem to make with people. As for me, it was always easy to make that instant connection with someone, but for that connection to stay and blossom into something more, was an unknown territory for me, I had lost hopes to ever get the chance to experience it. These thoughts were all I could think at times of desperation and need. There wasn't any effective path or thought process that I had developed to help me get out of this. Just a never-ending cycle from where I felt that I was all alone in this world.

However, I got an epiphany, where I realized the mere fact that I was comparing something as simple and true as friendship was what made my thinking go wrong. I finally realized that friendships happen due to various reasons and have different ends or continuations. None of it is something any of us can control. So, while my friendships didn't last as long as other people's seemed to last - that in no way points to the fact that they were any way less meaningful.

What actually mattered is that I made that connection with people and being with them taught me lessons that I would never want to forget. All those friendships were meaningful in their own ways and the fact that they ended isn't a testament to of them being wrong or not the right fit. All they pointed at, was that everything has an end and maybe their end was destined to be earlier than what other people's.

Even though, earlier I used to get this bitter feeling within me at the prospect of losing friends, they taught me that if I want these friendships to last longer, then there are steps that I too have to take. I can't always expect the other person to make the first move. All I had to do to make them last a little longer was to let go the elephant sized ego planted into my head and take that first step. If the other person wanted to continue they would too. If they didn't then at least I would know that maybe we just had reached the limit that was set for us and there was no room for regrets.

Now, the relationships that we have forged with others may end on a bad note or even leave us with a bitter afterthought due to reasons that we may not want to talk about. However, we should never ever regret the chance of getting to meet someone in our lives. No matter, what the outcome we may have faced, there are lessons that we have learnt from them and those can never be replaced. It is also something that has resulted in us being who we are today. And why would we want to be someone we aren't?

Other than the aspect of the length of our friendship, there is another very important aspect of having friends surrounding us, that is, to have people to rely upon at the times of need and despair. Group of people or any single individual that we seem to identify with, may be called as our "backbone." There are many times that I have heard from people about how they call themselves their own backbone. While there isn't anything wrong in doing this, we need to sometimes try to understand that we don't always need to have everything together. There isn't anything wrong in realizing the need of another person to help us through whatever tough times that we are going through. Though it still remains our fight, and others can help only to a certain extent, we should take whatever help we get from them.

I used to have this theory that says, I am all I will ever need. In some cases, that is what has proved to be a correct ideology to go by, but there are times where I would do anything to just know whom to call for help more than anything else in the world. However, I couldn't, because I was too scared to actually let someone in. All I did was hurt myself in order to avoid getting hurt. That seems like such a rubbish concept, but there are so many people I know who hide themselves behind this veil, always in the fear that they will get hurt when people leave or some other calamity will strike There have been times, when

I myself have told people that if we are too scared to be hurt again, we end up hurting ourselves. Inevitably, I myself couldn't actually believe in those words and go by them.

There is always one or the other fear that people always seem to associate themselves with, fears that have raised due to various insecurities, that in turn rise from the heart of a small instance, an insignificant crater in someone else's life, but because you are you, in a great way. I've usually found that in life, it is always the little things that end up mattering more to us than any other grand event that would took place. Most times, these changes are so minute, that we don't even realize it until its effect is over and at the end, we have come out as a different person from it.

As the insecurities that we have, results in having this innate fear that is more or less a part of us that we just don't know how to let go. This results in us being too scared to share, express or even get too close as we have already decided it in our heads that things are going to end badly. So, how do we prepare ourselves in this time of crisis? We all know that we can't predict what is going to happen in the future, but we continue to believe that everything is going to go wrong.

But have we just stopped and tried to think about these actions of ours: who are we to try to predict the outcome of the relationships we have and how badly it will end up leaving us being tattered in pieces. We need to try to and learn to accept that maybe it is going to be hard and it will be having such a horrible ending that we maybe shouldn't have started, but it might also end in something beautiful and serene that ends up being what we have always been looking for. The basic point here is that unless we have been gifted with this immense knowledge and powers to read the future and gauge the outcome of our lives, we should try to live our lives the way it is supposed to be dealt with and should not become an obstacle in the way of our own happiness.

Happiness can never be derived from anyone or anything, it just erupts when its need arises and return to its layers when its need may not be as eminent as earlier. So, letting people in, won't magically make all our problems disappear, it will to an extent give us an insight into what it feels like to know that you can fall back on someone.

There aren't any fixed boundaries on the extent to which we let people in as long as we are comfortable with how it is going. It is a gradual process but with the help of others, it does get some traction. There is this saying that I once heard from someone, "People can only help us in bringing our broken pieces together, it is our job to glue those pieces into a whole again."

INSECURITIES

Most of us are scared to show our true selves to the world in a fear of being judged. We feel the eyes of a crowd following our every move. The simple act of being who you are isn't even an option in your head as the question repeats, "what will people think?"

The number of people in the world who claim to be too scared of what people think of them has been too high to write about it as a simple problem. One of the deepest-rooted problems, all our insecurities rear their ugly heads in the first place due to our fear of being judged. The words and the way they are oriented may change, but the inner meaning behind them remains the same. The number of times I've heard those same words from people again and again- "what will people think"- makes me sick to my bones. And all I can understand from this is that people are too afraid to be themselves, though to be your own self should be our main priority.

Despite the fact that the society or the world we live in is ever-increasing and inhabits 7.5 billion+ people in the world. And if we are to make sure that none of our views, ideas or hopes clash with others, we are in for a world of difficulty. The only outcome we get by trying to make ourselves fit to others' ideas is making us unhappier, and even after going through this trouble there will still be another, maybe even bigger group, that is mocking us for those life choices. What is the point at the end then? Have we achieved even a single goal by adjusting our lives to the whims and fancies of others? The answer is no, and the earlier we realize that, that is all there to it, there are more chances of us being happy with ourselves.

However, in the face of this judgement, regardless of the fact that we let it affect ourselves or not, there is this feeling of not belonging that arises within us as we feel that people don't accept us as who we are.

So, the simple act of feeling comfortable in your skin doesn't come normally to people. Though I take pride of myself on not letting other's words affect me, never have I felt comfortable in my own skin. There's always this feeling that some foreign substance has taken a hostage into my body and is hiding my true self. It's been a prominent feeling as long as I remember. In my opinion, it's closely related to not having a sense of belonging, a common desire among everyone to feel belonged. But when we think about it what is this 'belonging' that we crave? Is it as simple as our need to be with our friends and feel included? Or does it run deeper within our bones, having to do more with the feeling, that we don't belong as the people we are?

A sense of belonging has always been an idea roaming in my head, I've always wanted to discover. On the days when I have no other thought roaming in my head, the feeling gets so strong that I feel as if I'm not part of the universe that I've inhabited. Thoughts roam my head as to how I'm an alien sent from an another planet living with humans that I have no connection with having no string that connects me to them. That was the only explanation that I could come up with as to why do I feel so secluded from everyone I know, why no matter how close I get to someone there's always this intense feeling of how it's me against the world. At times, I ponder, the reason as to why I can't let someone too close and the answer comes almost immediately - how can I let someone in when I don't belong to them. This idea has been fixed in my head for so long that I didn't know how to come out of it.

So, I continued to look for an escape, a distraction from this need to search for this 'belonging'. But what do I do when I sit alone at night and the thoughts that I have buried deep within the drawers of my head that no one has access to, fail to be kept inside. I can feel the urgency of these thoughts to break out from the reserves that I hide them in and when I let my guards down they come rushing in. At the end, I am consumed by these thoughts that refuse to get out and I'm left thinking all of those instances which left me feeling alone:

When I talk to the people, I call my closest friends and I can't understand why I feel that I'm not a part of them. How they are, who they are but when their joint laughter is all I can hear, I feel that the belonging I tried so hard to believe is there, was never there in the first place. It was all a figment of my imagination that I strived to achieve but failed to achieve in every sense.

When I can feel every inch of my body stating it with an extreme determination that this is not where I belong for reasons

I never know and no matter how hard I try I can't find an explanation.

What do you do when you face a situation? You feel the instances that led up to it but when it comes to explain those jumbled thoughts to anyone you know, you can feel your body shutting down and mere words are hard to form and you find yourself speechless. How does one develop the courage to utter the words, that are swirling in your head, to others when you have no idea how to start. This easy concept that others may not even spend a thought upon has been one of the hardest things I've had to overcome.

At times, I try to write it as a phase of my life that I will get over from. But what do you do when this phase has become the entirety of your life and you can't remember a time when you ever felt this 'belonging'. So, in the hope of making sense of this situation you try to find the logic in it, but what if your logic falls short in this one case. So, what do you do then?

Then you resort to something you don't think you're ready for, something you've tried to keep hidden to not let it cloud your judgement and your emotions. It may as well be the hardest thing you've done as you need to learn to tame the wild thoughts that threaten to unleash every time you let your emotions win over you. But you know, you are strong enough to achieve this Herculean task that you've always deemed impossible.

As you start realizing that the need of this 'belonging' is not as acute as you always thought it was, and you can feel hope seeping into your bones slowly. You realize how you may not belong to all the people around you but that doesn't mean that you're not part of this universe. Maybe, it means that you are the way you are to make yourself different from everyone else you know. There's something that separates you from the monotonous life that everyone else seems to be living. So, you might not belong to them but you do belong to yourself and that makes it a little easier to understand. You realize the comfort you sought from the outside world has always been inside you, you just didn't think of looking at it.

At times, you find yourself again falling back to the shell you tried really hard to stay out of, so you have hope in the future that maybe you'll find this 'belonging' but in the meantime you are who you are and there's no one else you'd rather be.

Just like me, there are so many people in the world dying to break out of their shells, their desire to delve into the deeper unknown grows every single day but at the some time they feel that there is a force that restricts them from doing the same. They don't realize that are harming themselves in a million ways by keeping their reserves of emotions deep within their hearts. They underestimate the need to let go of all the problems that haunt them and that can be done only when they decide to delve deep and find the cause hidden behind.

BELONGING

There is this feeling of belonging to one person. It's different from the general feeling of belonging that we think about, and sometimes it's what keeps people going forward and by not thinking about the past. It must be a really serene and peaceful feeling to acknowledge the fact that you have someone in your life, who you actually can't live without. Usually, this certain person is one you have given away your heart to and it is when you use the words, " you are in love." While there are many important relationships that one has in a lifetime, there is something that is present in this specific one that makes it different from everything else you have known.

Never honestly believing in it, love has always been a lost concept for me. While the people of my age seem to be falling in love, my attachment with this foreign concept had to offer was bordering on non-existent. I may have had an inkling to what this may entail from what I've seen in movies, books, or even my friends who can't seem to get enough of each other when they are in this haze. And though I had decided earlier on that this isn't something I would want , there are times when I am surrounded by people that are in love with each other. This just makes me feel a different type of loneliness that I have never felt before.

This isn't something where I feel no one is there for me, but it is something that raises this sad feeling within me of not having any person with me at that instant. The decision that I'm not meant for this still applies, but on my worst days where I'm just a constant "third-wheel" in my friends' lives, it wouldn't be so bad to have someone else along with me everyone has.

It isn't something I'm proud of, its something I keep hidden from the rest of the world. But what I desire is that just sometimes I don't want to feel alone in a group, and know that there is just this one person who will be there and as long as we both are there, neither of us will feel lonely, and that is all I want. Nothing extravagant, or any promises, but just the feeling of having someone right by your side.

Something as simple as this, but not something that I would honestly want for my life. I feel like I'm at crossroads, trying to find the right balance between what it is that I want with my life in a broader outlook, and what I sometimes want out of my life when I hit those moments where I don't know how to come out of them. At the end, this isn't something that I need to find the definition of, as time isn't making me rush in any way regarding this issue. It's just me and my thoughts that sometimes want more than what is being offered . In the wide view of things, this isn't something that requires any clear-cut meaning and maybe it's just one of the things in my life that maybe I experience and maybe I don't. No matter what it is, I am going to live my life the way I want to live it and at that moment, everything else just doesn't matter.

As long as you continue to do what it is that you are doing, everything will be fine and so will you be. While you may not get the one person to ease your loneliness in the way you desire, but you do have people in your life who love you more than anything else and that can keep you going as long as you require.

PARENTS

Maybe, people don't realize it but the type of relationships or friendships that a teenager makes as of now and the quality of those, depends to a large extent on the nature of our bonds with our parents. So, if the child is used to have an open, healthy relationship with their parents, the very same will be reflected on the friendships that they have with people around them.

The way we are and how we cope with situations thrown at our way depends mainly on this bond that we seem to neglect. Sometimes, parents say that they want to be their children's friends, but something that they don't realize is that friendship isn't a one-way street. If it is expected out of the child to treat their parent as their friend, the same should be true for the parents too.

In today's times the problems that a teenager goes through varies from something as simple as not having the right clothes to wear to something as serious as depression. Parents may not realize this, but the way a parent responds to any minute problem of the child is what will make the child decide whether to approach them when facing a tough situation. As it gets rooted in their head that if they weren't able to understand and accept my feelings about something that is very trivial, then how will they actually respond to something that makes all the difference in the world to them.

There is this constant fear of being judged that arises more from their parents than their friends or external environment as they have only one chance to understand what they are feeling and once they lose it there is no returning from that. When an honest and open relationship is wanted by one side, there is a need from the other side also to reciprocate the same.

There are various things that parents may overlook, but on the impressionable mind of the teenager it stays for as long as they will remember. Every time a child feels that their parents are never there for him/her literally or figuratively, his/her chances of bonding with his/her parent goes down. Every time the children feel their parents missed out on an important occasion of their life, the more let down they feel. Every time children try to reach out to their parents and express their emotions that they haven't been able to do for a long period of time and the parent turns them away, maybe unknowingly, the bond breaks further. Every time parents scream at their child, without knowing what is going on in the child's head, the more antagonistic she/he gets towards their parents. The more important a bond is, the more vulnerable it gets, and the parent child bond is something that needs to be preserved no matter what happens between them.

Teenagers may seem moody, emotional and a variety of other things that parents don't like, but what they require from them is their constant support and to feel as if their opinions do matter. A lot of people I know the teenagers in general always feel that their parents don't let them behave independently but want them to act that way. Although, when you think about it if a child is used to be micromanaged by their parents for every little thing that they do, how can they expect them to just magically become independent and be able to take major decisions on their own. If people expect us to act like adults, how can we do the same when our parents don't let us out of our shell.

There is a quote that my friend uses saying, "Parents aren't creatures of logic." Sometimes I feel that parents feel the same way towards us. So, when we delve deep into this issue, the only cause for it that can be found is that both sides are unaware on how to communicate with each other. Most times, I feel that if parents explain to their children why they are doing something instead of just saying it like an order, there is more probability of the teenagers listening to them. Let's take on example of something as simple as parents always telling children to study. If our parents actually sit down with us and say that they feel we should study so that we are ready for our future and know that we don't get anything easily in life without hard work and elaborate more on the point, the chances of us listening to them just increase.

So, maybe parents too think that we are too immature and won't understand anything. But if they give us an explanation as to why they want us to do a certain something, then there is an even higher chance of us to actually listening to them. This even makes the parents closer to the children, as people who respect each other.

When you think about it how many times do parents actually come up to their child and tell them that they are proud of them, that what they are doing is enough and they love them for who they are and always will. It may seem trivial , but it is something that every child needs to hear but doesn't get to hear and that results in them a feeling as if they aren't loved enough.

Teenagers are extremely egotistical people, so what we truly need is their parents to take the first step towards them and maybe their steps will be too slow in comparison to their, parents but they will reach there. As long as, we know that the path is open, there will come a time when teenagers will be ready to let in someone as important as their parents.

It is a human tendency to assign blame. Sometimes we do blame ourselves, but many times we end up coming up with excuses to blame others, just so that our conscience is clear. However, if we truly want to move on and close the gap that has been formed between our parents and us, we need to forego all the regrets and blames that we have kept deep within us. It may be hard and it isn't something that can be achieved just in a short amount of time. So we need to give ourselves time to let both parties get over their wounds and start everything from a clean slate. Both of us truly want to let go of the grudges that we have against each other. All we wait for is to see a clear sign from the other side that they too are ready to take that step, and then there will be nothing else that stands in the way.

CHAPTER 2

COMMUNICATION

"The single biggest problem in communication is the illusion that it has taken place."

-George Bernard Shaw

There is this inexplicable power that is present in words. It isn't something that I have always thought or believed in for that matter, but lately as I have been introduced to all the benefits that it has to offer, there is this immense power that I feel within me. This can even be correlated to one of the reasons that I admire in authors. It seems unfair, viewing the amount of influence they have in making us feel things. The way they make us feel what they want us to feel, to render the whole world invisible to us as we imagine ourselves in the world that they have created and made us lose ourselves in it. People may not think twice of it, but recently this is all I can think about. There is this feeling of wanting to do the exact same thing that they do.

There is this quote that has stayed in the back of my head for a long time, the source from where I'm not very sure,, but all I know is that it has left me reeling at its importance. It went something like this, "Actions are temporary, words stay forever."

That is something I haven't ever been able to forget, that makes me realize the importance that simple words possess and how maybe instead of chasing, after proving things by our actions, we should concentrate upon.

Though I will not say that actions are somewhat useless, but I do believe that in the fight of words against actions, maybe in more than one case we should choose words. We all seem to romanticize the notion of actions by asserting that we reach a point where we feel the need for people to know what we are going through without ever saying it out loud. In some instances, maybe that is exactly what happens. But we need to realize that sometimes people close to us can't read our minds, that no matter how well they do know us, maybe our actions say otherwise. All that is failing us at that instant aren't the people around us, but just the lack of us effectively communicating with others to get the message across as we want it to be.

If we look back at our life, how many instances can we conjure up where maybe a relationship had ended because we weren't open with the idea of letting the other person know what we truly felt by saying it out, or how many times did we reach a stalemate in an argument because either of the side wasn't ready to express effectively? The reason for it is something simple. There is this fear to speak out what we want others to desperately know, so in the process we feel it is easier if the other person guesses it for us That may be the case in certain situations, but if we really want others to know what we are feeling we need to speak it out. Maybe it isn't what we wanted it to be and doesn't give us as much satisfaction as we wanted, but it does help in knowing that one person out there knows what it is that we desperately want in the world. We need to learn to accept that we can feel better, if just we allow ourselves to do it by using these ever-altering words.

If we look back at our life and think about the instances when simple words had left us breathless, or feeling as if our heart would blast from the amount of happiness that we felt then we will understand what I'm trying to say here. We shouldn't let ourselves be slaves of our actions and let it bind us to a spot with nowhere else to go, instead we should open ourselves to this exhilarating experience that has the power to change us all for the better only if we allow it to.

TECHNOLOGY

Technology has advanced to such a great extent that the difference between someone miles away from us and someone who lives right next to us is almost nonexistent. We are living at an age where connection has become the most important thing in our lives. No matter where we are or who we are, if we don't belong to a social networking site like Facebook it is impossible to actually stay connected to the world. The actions of people that we know nothing about can be known by just a click of the button. We've developed a sort of addiction,where we feel this explicit need to broadcast all our needs and feelings to the outer world. The people we meet or the places we go are all announced for reasons that I'm not sure we know ourselves.

While I'm not implying that there is anything wrong in doing anything that someone wishes to do, I want people to actually think about what their actions are leading to and think of the reasons why we are doing it. We are so connected to the outside world, so why do we feel so lonely ourselves? Isn't the whole point of getting connected to people is that we don't feel lonely, but is that actually working? I know people who besides being really "connected" still feel a strong sense of being disconnected, and I myself have felt this detachment from the rest of the world many times.

Even if we look at just the connection that we have formed with people throughout, the question we should be asking ourselves is that even if we do feel we are connected to the world throughout; do we actually know the people we talk to? Do we know the way the person actually is? What their favorite color is, their likes and dislikes or their unusual mannerisms? The question we should ask ourselves is that in this super connected world do we know why someone is the way they are?

At times like this, where our disconnection to ourselves and the people that really matter is greater than ever before, we should leave our devices to themselves and venture out into the unknown. Leave the connections that we try to form with people through emoji and texts and instead try to get to know the person at face value. That is when we feel that we actually know someone and feel the connection that we've always craved.

LISTENING

Keeping in mind the ways words can truly help someone or even us, we shouldn't forget another important facet of communication: listening.

Have we sometimes thought that we seem to have conversations with ourselves despite the fact that others are there with us? That the difference between the conversation that we are having with others and saying the same words in front of a wall is - only the presence of another person in our room? Maybe you won't get what I'm saying, so think back to the deep conversations that you have with your friends, where you talk about the things that you may not have normally talked about. In those instances, can you remember something that your friend may have disclosed that he/ she may have been struggling deeply with, but in our need to respond, we don't actually think about what he/she is saying means to her?

Conversations basically points to two people voicing out their own opinions/ talking about a certain instance. This is where we supposedly listen to each other, but do we actually listen? There is a thin line between hearing something and listening and more often than not, we seem to do the former. Where the words that are spoken by the other, is a sound that is picked up by our ears, but we are not even close to register the words that they are speaking, and say just what we want.

There is this saying that I had read before says, "humans listen to respond not to understand." When I read this, I actually realized what I have been doing during my whole life. While I seemed to "listen" to what the other person has to say to me, but only for the reason so that I can say what is there on my mind, and sometimes I don't even register what exactly they are trying to say and continue saying what I wanted to say.

Do you also feel that way, where you continue stringing words along, while not registering what the other person is saying and they continue to do the same?

This has made me realize a grave mistake that I had been committing throughout my life. Now I get that sometimes, there is a way in which two people communicate to each other, while speaking what is there on their mind by not explicitly responding to said person's thoughts. Maybe that is an actual conversation but what we resort to at times is each side's conversation happening in a different frequency with no connection to someone else. It makes me feel that we are actually living in a lonely world, where we all are actually just fending for ourselves, where we may think that we do but actually don't care about people the way we should.

If we think of it rationally and look back, we will realize that all the words people around us say have a reason, and sometimes we should look deeply at those words and realize that maybe they are giving their own calls of help and we are just ignoring them without even realizing it. This doesn't mean that I have suddenly become the most attentive and best listener in the world, but it is a course that I have stepped into, to come out as a better person and even though I keep getting setbacks on my way, I won't stop until I have reached my goal.

It should make us think about what type of people we want to be, one that only listens to our own thoughts or the one who is there for others.

Let us actually practice this art of "listening" and try to master it instead of just delving on the useless act of "hearing" what others have to say.

HELPING OTHERS

An internal desire to help is something that is within all of us. The intensity of this desire might be different, but that doesn't go on to say that it isn't present. It rises out one of the simplest and purest of acts, something selfless that we do, without any hope of it being reciprocated. As in that moment, all we care out is lending a helping hand to one that desires it and the only objective that is present in our mind is to help the said person out of their difficulties. It isn't something that you could explain on a cellular level, but I have my own (maybe inconsistent) theories: there is some hormone that gets released on knowing that said person is happy and the reason is you. The fact that you can impart happiness to people (no matter how minimalistic) is what helps you through the toughest times.

In a way of speaking, this "selfless" can't exactly be connoted as selfless due to the fact that we do have a motive behind doing it. It may not be something devious or cruel but what motivates us is the fact that helping the said person gives us happiness too in its own way, and we will continue to do the same in hopes of getting to experience that head rush as many times as we can.

It is very easy to impart advice but to actually take it into account in our own life sometimes borders on the impossible. There are reasons as to why the same happens, but at the end this isn't something that we can just deem reasonable as this defies all logic. Whenever faced with any problem, it seems to become rooted in our heads, we feel it closing in around us. This is when we require external help as others aren't limited by the same boundaries as we are, they can effectively pull us out of those closed doors and help us see the world in their way.

This is in its rudimentary form what takes place, but in the real world, it isn't as easy as that. As there is a line that one has to draw between helping someone and forcing them to see what you can see very clearly. I have learnt this little late but nonetheless as I have encountered such experiences with people all around me. When this happens, in the place of that addictive head rush is just a disappointment, disappointment of not being good enough to help the person to see what you want them to see. Even worse at not being able to do anything about it.

This is a time when you can see the person breaking down right in front of your eyes and there isn't anything that can be done from your side to help them. You've tried time and time again, and you feel yourself coming short on them in more than one occasion. But this isn't something that you can just quits as, if the person had done the same you wouldn't be here anymore. It isn't even a form of exchange that you are playing at, you do it genuinely without any motive as the only thing that you can care about at that moment is that the person has to get out of whatever situation they're facing. You are going to do whatever is there within your power to help them.

There are various things that you could do, but one that is strictly out of the picture is forcing the other to talk, as if you start from there, nothing can be achieved by you and you will not be able to help them either. There are times that the helplessness of the situation drives you crazy and all you can think about is shaking the person with all your might in a hope that they can see what you are seeing. But that is as good as waving the white flag in front of them, as the tiny hope that they had on you would have evaporated like a cloud.

So, instead of thinking about it emotionally and not going anywhere, you decide to go about it logically.. To take part in such a process, it can't happen all at once or at the moment, it is a process of an observation that you have to engage in order to understand what is it that would help the said person through it what is the person like, what helps them when they are dull, what doesn't help. One should actually listen to them instead of just hearing their words and trace back to the words that they might have spoken at that point to how to help them and that is how we get our base ready. It may as well be classified as an army strike or attack due to the amount you have prepared.

Even when you have reflected on the person and got certain ideas ready,what you have to engage in, is the deliberate act of being there for them and them knowing that you are there. It has to be in the subtle ways that you express it to them, but they should know that you are right there with them, no matter what they go through. As this develops, make them more comfortable to share what it is that they're going through little by little..

Slowly and gradually maybe they do get better, maybe they don't, but if a decision has been made by you to help them and be there for them, then that is a decision that you have to stick to, no matter what weather you face. It is a commitment that has been created and there is no "out" that you can seek in the middle of it all. If we do decide to stay along the ride for them, then the fact that we have helped out someone truly should be a present for us.

Through all this, something that we sincerely need to comprehend is that in the end this is their battle, not ours and we need to let them learn their own way out of this problem. As this is a journey that they have to go through and we need to just let them know that we are there for them: for the good and the bad, and we aren't going anywhere anytime soon.

LETTING OTHERS HELP US

In this process of helping others, there is something else that we should keep in mind. It is the power present in people to make us believe that we believe in them. There is this unique power that people hold over us to change how we think and who we are, if we just allow ourselves to be open enough to listen to what it is that they have to share. People can move mountains in front of us, but unless we truly believe in its possibility, nothing is going to change within us. However, that being true, if we just try to really listen to what it is that people have to say to us instead of already making it up in our head, then there is a real possibility to change us for the better.

But most times, when we are enlisting others help we don't take their words to heart and don't understand what it is that they are trying to tell us. There aren't any reasons that can be pinpointed to why this happens. All that is known by us is that this is the normal human nature, something that can't be avoided.

So, as we continue in this path of hearing but not actually listening to what it is that they have to say to us, all we feel is that people's words don't seem to provide the help that is needed to overcome what we are going through.. While it is true, that we are the only ones who can truly help ourselves see the light that others try so hard to show, it doesn't mean that others can't be helping hands. There is a bridge that they form and it clearly links us to the points of our destination, and if we listen and actually absorb the words and believe what they are saying, then the chances of it helping us see the light increases exponentially.

This may seem idealistic, and maybe it is, but this can actually happen and I have experienced the same myself. I have been on both sides of the spectrum and what I can truly say is that if we just give them the chance, the positivity that it brings us won't let anything stand in our way. There is a difference that we will observe when we seem closed to what others have to say and when we willingly accept what they are trying to tell us. If we are aware that we can feel better and can look at the world differently only if we open our eyes and let it, then isn't that a chance that we should willingly take? What is it that we have to lose if we don't succeed? We have everything to gain if we just accept it.

Maybe this will open up expectations and chances of disappointment, and that very truly is what life is. We can't rest all our hopes on another person so that we don't feel the way we do, but the number of times that it would help us, will be much more than when it would not and that makes it all worthwhile in the end.

DIFFERENT WAYS TO HELP

While talking about the very ways in which communication can help others, there is something that we should keep in mind: the extent to which communication can help if we just focus on one of the multiple ways to behave as our outlet.

It has always been hard to articulate all the thoughts that run in my head into words that can be spoken to another person, and much easier to just write it all down with the utmost detail. They all are usually jumbled thoughts with words stringed together to form barely coherent sentences, but they usually left me with this content feeling that I was able to say all that I needed to say, even if it was on a piece of paper. A paper that contained words I could never say out loud, away from the watchful eyes of everyone I knew.

I remember forming points regarding all that I needed to say to a certain, someone, putting it all in my head and making sure that I would go forward with it, being sure that I would say all that was needed to say without a doubt. However, I vividly remember never being able to actually say what I needed to say, leaving out all the important points that I had molded in my head with the utmost certainty, only to not have the courage to say it out loud. Words spoken from the mouth always failed me. The words that seemed to be at the tip of my tongue just couldn't dare to come out and instead spent time swirling throughout my head and my tongue, only to be disappointed and make its way back to where it came from.

What is it that stopped me from saying the words those I deeply wanted to say, was a question that was left unanswered. All I knew that writing those same words was a feat that I could undertake, but saying it out wasn't even an option. I still remember the days where all the things that I wanted to let out, thoughts and feelings that kept piling inside my heart and head to form their very own mountain, demanded to be left out. There wasn't even a choice that I could make, as the very notion of saying what I wanted to say to another party wasn't even part of the discussion, leaving me with only one way out: writing it all down; realizing that where the spoken words had failed me, maybe the unsaid written ones won't. To a certain extent they didn't, there was so much that I wanted to let out and it became a sort of tradition to write whatever it is that I wanted to express As long as I could get it out in some ways.

You may say that I secured those pages in an iron lock within me, the keys to which wasn't something that anyone else had the power to hold, and neither would I let them. However, unfortunately without my knowledge, the lock must have been picked because people whom I desperately didn't want to know how I felt, happened to get the chance to read exactly that in that moment, and all I could feel was a part of me disintegrating. The only medium for expression that I had the honor of finding, had been taken away from me. Maybe, there is a part of me that is exaggerating the effects that it held over me, as it wasn't something that I was ridiculed over or even spoken to. But, just the knowledge of knowing that something that I had desperately wanted to keep away from the rest of the world had ended up exactly the opposite way, left me devastated.

Writing them was the one way I had to cope with what I was feeling but had no way of comprehending. When I lost that, there wasn't anything that I knew I could do to actually feel better. I subconsciously developed this fear within me to express anything I went from constantly writing what I was feeling to trying to not even think about what it was that I was feeling.

However, I found the light at the end of the tunnel. It came in the form of writing, similar to what I had done before, but with the intention of writing a book. All the fears that resided within me regarding people, knowing exactly what it was that I was feeling, seemed to vanish. There was still this fear right before showing the same to someone about what they would think. But it wasn't something that left me paralyzed, instead it fueled me to write even more, dig deeper and find what it was that I was feeling. Realizing the possibility of helping even a single person, for them to know that they aren't all alone, no matter what happens, assuaged all my fears.

There is this realization that happened through this process, something that taught me more than any other experience could. That we all have different methods of dealing with situations. Something that helps one person, doesn't necessarily help the other and that's the way the life is. But something that we need to do, as we live in this jumbled mess we seem to call life is to find out something that helps us deal with the demons we face. We can't deny the fact that we all have demons those we are trying to slay and sometimes all we need to do is to find an outlet.

CHAPTER 3

PRESSURE

"Mistakes and pressure are inevitable; the secret to getting past them is to stay calm."

-Travis Bradberry

When you look back to a time that changed you to the very core of your existence:

That deep chill that creates an unsettling feeling throughout your bones! You feel something is ringing in your ears and the next thing you know is that you're throwing up all the contents of food you've eaten in the past 24 hours. You know what resulted in the initiation of this chain reaction but you feel as if you don't have the courage to think about it yourself, much lesser talk to someone about it. So, that's where you find yourself – crying and puking out your guts where an end to this life that you're living, doesn't seem in sight. You don't want to live like this anymore in this never-ending cycle that you've found yourself trapped into. All you can do is just hope for something to stop this hamster cycle that your life has become.

Looking back and thinking about what kick started this very reaction, one phrase comes to your mind. A phrase that people ask what you're going through. A phrase that has the potential to explain the reasons as to why you are going through this. Regardless of the accuracy of this phrase, something within you never let you accept the reality you are facing and you just continue to live in your own bubble of denial. You find yourself hoping against hope that you prove everyone else wrong and prove that this isn't real.

Slowly, with no other solution that makes sense you start accepting what you're going through and you utter the words to finally accept what is happening: you feel as if the pressure of the world is upon your shoulders.

No one in the world is born with this pressure; It's simply a transformation that you go through that makes you change from a carefree individual to someone who isn't able to deal with even minor obstacles thrown at their way. Simply put, it arises due to the pressure put on you by other people that manifests itself inside you in such a way that even in the absence of this external pressure, you feel as if you've been living inside a pressure cooker that has far surpassed its limits.

There are a lot of reasons that result in people to go through something like this. For me personally, it was due to the pressure that I felt I was living under. It got to a point where before I even start something there a hundred other things that run through my mind about whether I will be able to go through this or not, how much effort I have to put in, what will happen if I am not able to achieve the goal that I have set for myself and it keeps going so on . The only purpose it served was to ruin my chances of achieving what I want to achieve and nothing else. All I could hear were the voices in my head chanting that I couldn't do this; I couldn't do that , with no knowledge as to how to make them stop.

As time passed, the pressure to be perfect kept increasing, and so did the feeling that I was making everyone disappointed to the point where it wasn't something that I could just deal with. Something I'm still ashamed of is the unhealthy outlet that I found for the situation that I was facing. It was something that I did very subconsciously, and it involved me ruining my own health. Sadly, it had become somewhat of a daily occurrence for me, and even though I denied it for as long as two months, somewhere in the back of my head I knew what people who called me being stressed, were actually true.

I hoped for there some other reason to be there for me being this way. Some medical anomaly could would explain why my stomach was acting up so much, but I was just in denial. Denying the fact that I wasn't normal like every other person I knew, who could deal with tough situations on their own without puking their guts out and staying at home in seclusion from the rest of the world. However, as the various tests results came back negative, the likelihood of what everyone was telling me seemed to be truer than ever before. After a point, I'm pretty sure no one believed in me anymore, nor did I believe in the web of lies I was trying to live in.

As days passed, I did get better and then not better any further and it seemed as if I would never be able to get out of this cycle. The days when I felt as if I relapsed were my worst, where no one could understand the loss of hope and life, I felt when I was stuck in this situation. I was tired of people telling me how I should look at the "bright side." There was no bright side that I could see anymore, only a sense of emptiness that I guessed had become what I would call my life. Every time I made a setback on my progress, I hit my lowest point. Nonetheless, every time I made it out of this maze, I felt I was recovering and there was this feeling that there is hope for me, and no matter how bad situations get I can make it out of this.

I remember breaking down in front of my friend with absolute despair at not knowing how to continue from this point onwards. That was the day that I accepted what I was going through and I've never looked back since then.

Slowly but gradually, I did start making progress, I remember counting the number of days that I could go without puking and every time I broke a new record. The happiness I felt was unparalleled. People didn't understand this and I didn't need them to,as this was my own battle and I was winning it in the best way I could.

This experience taught me a lot, and one of the main things that I learnt from this was that you don't always need to be strong and independent to go through everything in your life on your own. Everyone needs people that give them moral support and are there to share the burden that they feel. You have to be strong enough on your own to go through a situation, but having people along for the ride makes it a little easier to go through. They don't always need to understand what you're going through as the chances of them going through something exactly same are pretty low, but that doesn't mean you shouldn't let them in, just because you fear that no one gets it.

People may not understand many things which we go through and we need to accept that. As no matter, how alone we may feel we are in life, that is never what the case actually is.

Another thing I learnt from this was that I couldn't just keep blaming the group of people which I felt always pressurized me as they might have been the ones who t started this process for me to strive to be perfect, but it is me , who continued it with my own thoughts and my goals. So how could I blame someone for doing the exact same thing as I was doing? I feel we always have this desire to blame people for all the bad things that happen in our life. Even if it makes us feel better in some ways, it doesn't let us move on from the situation that we are experiencing and thus it doesn't even let us grow.

MISTAKES

Make or break. Make or break. Every little decision that we have ever faced always comes down to us with a feeling that this is what will define how our lives will plan out to be. The dilemma that we face for even the little things can be all boiled down to the fear that we feel that we are making the wrong decision and who knows where this so called wrong decision will take us. Sometimes it may originate from the lack of trust that we place in ourselves and sometimes it may even be due to some untoward reason that we may as well never get to know. At the end, does it all really matter? It's a point we reach where we need to excel at everything we do with no room for mistakes.

There isn't any option that we have left for ourselves to let us learn from the past mistakes. We may have experienced losses once or twice, but at least I feel that we haven't let ourselves swallow the bitter pill of failure to help us learn how to overcome failures and rise from there. I don't feel anyone really talks about how important failure can actually constitute in someone's life and thus as a result, we all need to win. We have created a mentality where if we are actually into something and we have put in all our efforts, there is no other option other than winning and while that may make us super competitive and successful in a few cases, it also doesn't prepare us for the life that we are getting ready to live: filled with chances of failures along the road and there isn't anything that we can do to change that very fact.

Our need to be correct all the time, makes us worry and over analyze what sort of decision we should take. However, we do not realize that we will never learn the difference between right and wrong, if we never make a mistake. The only end result we will face if we continue to lead this way is a life which continues to be indecisive no matter where we go.

We may have noticed that our parents are always worried about us making mistakes and try to go out of their way to make sure that we don't. Maybe this irrationality of theirs has come down to us. But when trying to look at this in another perspective, what we don't realize is that making mistakes is the most natural part of being human, and if we have never faced any such mistakes there is no room for us to grow as people.

People always say learn from your mistakes. However, when there is no room for mistakes in our lives , where will we learn from? It may sound obnoxious or something really obvious, but if it is one of the most obvious things in the world then why aren't we able to apply it in the situations that we face?

I never actually tried to sit and understand what this really meant until someone once talked to me about how in today's age, kids aren't used to failure. That is when I realized that we've been so tuned to really try for something and achieve what we want that we forget that the need to learn something new is more important than "succeeding" any feat. While this attitude of ours may be considered good in certain cases, we aren't prepared to actually know how to deal with a major setback in our lives .Now for us, small failures are considered as major setbacks in life like not getting good grades or not winning any competition, etc. While these may be considered as failures, for the life that we are preparing ourselves, we are nowhere even close to getting ready. As how will we know to actually pick ourselves up after a major accident that may have the potential to change the course of our lives when we have no idea how to move on from a minor setback.

I myself have been oblivious to the true meaning of failure until recently. There had been a lucky spell in my life I could say, where whatever I tried I was able to do really good at. It may not have been great things but for me I was really happy with the fact that as I was putting in effort, I was able to achieve the goals that I had set for myself and I couldn't be happier.

However, recently I went through an instance where I had to deal with failure almost every day. I realize this may sound stupid or insignificant to some people but it actually impacted me in ways I didn't even realize. SAT and ACT examinations are an integral step one has to take, when they are trying to go abroad for further studies and like many others, I also have been trying to "crack" these exams. A lot of my friends have given this test earlier and when I used to hear from them about the hardships they faced while giving this test, I never truly understood it until now. I personally thought I would be able to become better overnight and felt the effort I'd put in was more than enough to get better at this, oh and boy was I wrong.

The true meaning of failure is what I realized when I had to give practice tests after practice tests and in none of them was I able to get even a decent score that was acceptable for any institute. The let downs that I had everyday started affecting me so much that I could feel all of it getting to my head. Everyday a sense of dread spread across me at realizing that this was what my life had become to and a question kept popping in my head - "how come I am not able to excel at this when I'm trying." That's when I realized that I had got too comfortable with the prospect of winning and now I didn't know how I could effectively work around this setback and then try to prosper from it.

This went on for weeks altogether and as the setbacks increased, my effort reduced and all I could feel was disappointment for not being able to do good in this so called "easy" test. It can be said that I reached rock bottom one day (, and that is when I got the push that was really needed. The words of others that usually fell on deaf ears, now were inclined to listen to what others had to say. I transferred their energy within, and I could feel myself saying that I could do it. The confidence that wasn't there at any level earlier, was now filled inside me and I knew I could do this. People seemed surprised at this new-found confidence that I seemed to have got and all I could say was that I could feel myself rising and getting ready to wage this battle with something as small as this examination.

This instance ended up being a very thought-provoking one for me, making me question how we all live our lives without trying to learn something from it.

It made me think; does our need to never be wrong still seem reasonable? Or are we starting to realize the irrationality of our ways? All we can hope is for us to learn from the mistakes that seem to plague us all year around.

This isn't an indication for us to just keep making mistakes and say that we are just learning from it. The only claim I make, is for us to not let this simple act of making a decision the hardest thing in our lives . All we need to learn is that the decisions we make, either right or wrong doesn't matter, like everything else in life it depends upon what the process teaches us about ourselves, while giving us a chance to grow and prosper in life, in whatever way we may want to.

ACT OF COMPARING

The overused line that we all are unique actually has a very fundamental theory to it: the fact that all the chromosomes have combined in different permutations to form who we are, makes us all different. We all need to take extreme measures to fix this thought in our head, to realize that at the end, we all are different: from things as simple as to our eating habits to the type of values that are instilled in us.

In the sea of vast differences, there is this human tendency to always think that others are better, where we feel that if someone is better than us in one activity that automatically means that they have something, we lack and thus a decision is made by us that they are better than us. Sometimes, we may want to become like someone else or want the life that they are living, or we may not exactly want their lives but there is this tiny tinge of jealousy rising within us to want to have, what the other has .

It's a kind of a one-dimensional thought process we have, we look at what the others supposedly possess and we don't; could t it be an accessory or some talent that they have, and that makes us feel how blessed they are, unlike us. What we truly fail to take into account is that no one can have all of it. While some people may be good at the things that "really matter," there are a mountain load of other feats where, we are much better off than them.

There are so many people out there comparing themselves to others, and that isn't something that can be just stopped. As comparison is something, that is inherent in all of us and doesn't have anything to make us stop doing the same, while we are comparing ourselves to others we need to learn how to be objective. In that sense, when we are comparing ourselves to others, we should do that by keeping in our mind what we want out of life and what they do, and thus similarly where each of our's interest levels lie. When we look at it from our logical lens instead of our emotional ones, then this act of comparison isn't something that will bring us sadness, instead it will give us the objectivity that we require and we might even learn a few things from it.

CHAPTER 4

THE PERIOD OF CHANGES

"I am not a product of my circumstances. I am a product of my decisions."

-Stephen Covey

We all go through this phase in our lives where, who we didn't use to be isn't who we are right now. It simply means that the person we were at the young age of twelve or thirteen; isn't who we have become at this age. It may be a chain reaction to a certain huge incident, or the culmination of small events and thoughts that have mixed in a certain proportion in order to change us into whom we are today. The ability to exactly pinpoint when or how this started isn't something that is very clear to us, the only thing we know for sure is that it happens to all of us.

Throughout this process, there isn't any inclination that what we are going through is wrong, as change is inevitable. No matter who we are, we learn to adapt to the environment that we are facing or the changes that happen within us. It's hard to be okay with this change that we face, but that doesn't mean we won't be able to familiarize with it. Human beings can adjust to whatever situation that they face, no matter how big or small.

What makes it hard is that the transition that we go through isn't apparent to the world outside us. It's usually the change in our thoughts and perception towards life that is hidden from the rest of the world. The reason for this transition differs from person to person with the only thing being in common is the end result - a different version of us.

The only way to truly comprehend and actually move on from this period of everlasting changes is by trying to trace back to the events, from where there is a possibility that this rose from.

It may be a period in your life that occurs when you have detracted from your path and may have delved into activities that you aren't fully aware of. An activity for which you haven't exactly gathered the intelligence to be aware of, but something, that has been unofficially classified as a rite of passage in every teenager's life. It's a time where people drink and participate in other activities usually not for the sake of forgetting, but maybe to fit into the group that they belong to. It starts of, as something that you want to try out with a person close to you, away from the eyes of the known ones you know. A feeling of "high" that you experience, makes you feel that you have reached the level of being proclaimed as "drunk". However, as times change and maybe so does your group, you get introduced to people that partake in this activity on a weekly basis. You first try out a little to fit in and not seem as the odd one out of the group. But slowly, your desire to try more and more increases and the word 'no' seems to not exist in your dictionary anymore. You cover the fact that you have been increasing your intake to an unhealthy level by saying that you do it to forget about the problems that you face. However, not realizing that all it does is bringing up everything that you were trying to forget. As this continues, there is only one slip up that is needed to make all hell break loose. A slip up that no one could have foreseen and a time where you were having fun turns to you slipping from the stairs and falling in the pool of your own blood in the blink of an eye.

The next thing you know you wake up at the hospital bed with no recollection of where you are and what happened. And at that moment you no longer remember the person you were earlier .

That is, when who you are - a question that you seem to have no answer to. As at this moment, who you are and what you do are two phenomena that don't seem to intersect..

Other than this normal rite of passage that leaves most teenagers with no idea of who they are, some people go through another type of transition.

I recall once meeting a girl named Sahana, who told me that she didn't know who she was anymore. I was baffled by this statement of hers, but the more I heard her story, more I understood her predicament.

She said that she had become the exact opposite of the person she used to be. Elaborating on the story she spoke about her childhood, about how she used to be the bubbly and outspoken girl, who would never back down from a fight. I saw the dazed look on her face, as she was recollecting about those times while speaking about the girl she used to be. Fighting until her last breath and never taking 'no' for an answer were her strong traits.

However, being brought up in an orthodox Hindu family, her sharp tongue was a source of irritation for her entire family. She was ridiculed for being the way she was, again and again. Either it was behind closed doors or in front of the whole world to see. Nevertheless, nothing was able to break the indomitable spirit that she was born with. But despite her best efforts after a matter of time, it all got up to her. She wasn't able to take the constant humiliation due to the fact of who she was-.

They wanted her to follow the guidelines they had set for her, for her to fit into this shell they had built and for her to never to break out of it. After saying things that she felt and meant in every nice way possible, and on the off chance that it hurt one of the very prideful people of her family she was to be reprimanded again and again until she stopped saying anything that she wanted to say, stopped even thinking of expressing herself anymore. She finally realized there is no point in speaking your mind when all it's going to do is harm yourself and the people around.

Gradually, she transformed from a girl who never backed down to someone who forgot how it felt like to speak up, she became someone who just let everyone walk over her because the fear of confrontation that embedded deep within her wasn't something that she could just let go. The terror that seized her every time she thought of trying to just voice her opinion left her paralyzed, forgetting how it felt like to move or speak, and all she could do instead was to choose the easiest way out - not saying anything.

I remember feeling so helpless after listening to her recount and tried to imagine how the young Sahana was able to go through this without anyone by her side. She tried to act composed and didn't show her vulnerable side but despite her best efforts, I could see a tear run down her face. I contemplated telling her to stop, but I realized she needed to let it all out.

Continuing a moment later, she spoke about the transformation that she underwent. Speaking about the helpless nights and days that she went through, when all she wanted was for it to stop but didn't know how. At the end, the endless days became years and who she used to be, became a distant dream.

So how does someone return from that? How do they rebuild their identity from the remains of who they used to be? Is it possible or is it something that is so incomprehensible that there is no point, even in trying? There is no way to come up with a plausible answer to these questions. It's something that we need to decide on our own: are we ready to let life walk all over us or are we going to fight back?

There is this flight or fight hormone in our body that gets activated when faced with situations of extreme difficulty. It's what that decides either are we will go to fight the problem that we've faced or we will chose to run away from it. It applies in all situations, even when we need to make a split-second decision.

In Sahana's case, she could have decided to just wait for some external force that would change her life to how it used to be or she could actively take part in trying to change her path into something that she wanted, to fight it instead of just rolling over. She decided to take the path filled with more difficulties but realized it was worth it as she could reach the goal that she wanted to achieve. It wasn't something that happened all at once, she took it in one day at a time. There was no desire within her to accelerate the process, all she wanted was help from anyone who was ready to give her.

I soon realized that the help she required wasn't in the traditional sense; she didn't need me to be her anchor. All she needed was someone to show the way for hope, someone to help her rise it within her again. I remember seeing improvements in her, small subtle changes that would go unnoticed to the naked eye but on close inspection, you could see her attempts to change.

The change was evident in the way she started voicing her opinions and dreams in the confines of a room to someone she treasured close to her heart. Slowly but gradually, how she started gathering the courage to say "no", a word so simple but having a powerful effect, when she felt her needs were being sacrificed. Finally, she learnt to put herself before anyone else, realizing that it didn't make her selfish but stronger. She was able to delve into the pools of strength that were hidden deep within her but were lost somewhere.

The concept of identity became a variable in her life that she didn't feel the need to define it. She is, who she is, not a product of her circumstances but a product of her decisions and as far as decisions go, she was as proud of herself as one could be. Sahana is a source of inspiration to everyone in the world who feels the need to know what their identity is. She gave me hope in realizing that no matter what situation one goes through, one can always bounce back from it with more force and determination than they initially did.

What this points to is that it is due to transition that the question of who we are becomes blurry to us. All of us have this image of ourselves in our head related to the ideals that we feel we should always uphold. So when we come to the conclusion that we aren't able to uphold those ideals/actions anymore, is when our sense of identity becomes unclear as how do you know who you are when you've become this completely new person that you don't identify with anymore. Getting to know who you are, is very important, especially to every teenager out there, who finds himself/ herself in this place of identity crisis where they don't know how to continue doing what they do until they get a clearer picture of who they are.

Both these instances though caused by different reasons,

the way to move on from them is the same- to learn to accept the new you.

The need to develop this identity doesn't always have to be caused by a traumatic accident, sometimes it arises due to change. Change is inevitable, but that doesn't necessarily mean that we are ready to accept it. Teenagers go through a very dramatic change throughout their lives where the image of who they thought they are, and who they can develop into, are extremely contrasting. We feel we're disappointing ourselves by not holding up the ideals we've set. That is when our identity crisis tends to start and people suffer an identity crisis throughout the world. The question of who they are, haunts them on a daily basis.

Identity as a general concept is very absurd, something that we all crave but don't know how to achieve. Some say it is associated with your name. As your name is something that makes you unique, helping you differentiate yourself from a crowd. But what if your name is not something you identify with? Instead is something that has been forced upon you and has failed to deliver the job of serving as your identity? If your name could be anything within the crowd and you won't know how it makes you any different or unique from anyone else you've known.

It's a normal human nature wanting to know who we are and what our purpose is and with time we'll be able to figure out a way to find something that serves as a medium to help us bridge the gap between us and our unknown identity.

TIME

In wake of such transitions, the only way to truly move on from a place where we have no knowledge of who we are, is by giving it time. Though we always think of it as such a fixed state; however, it is the most fleeting thing that we'll ever experience. Time never waits for anyone, we all know this, but to actually believe in it is a whole together another matter. Everything we go through, always seems like the end of the world, the moments when we are at our lowest point, always seem to drag endless and we feel that we'll never ever be able to get over this feeling. Even when we tell ourselves, that we need to get over something , it doesn't necessarily mean that we actually believe in it.

As we look back at our lives , all the hard moments that we've gone through where we felt we wouldn't be able to survive it, we realize that we did go through it. We may not have been aware, but with time our wounds did heal and so did we. Slowly, but capably, we began to make ourselves whole again and our composition today may be completely different from what it used to be, but we accept ourselves for being us, no matter how we are or who we are.

A friend of mine, Anaya once told me about a time in her life where everything seemed uncertain. She had just graduated from tenth and was changing schools and was trying to get into various other good, prestigious schools. At this time, her dad had not been happy with his job and thus, decided to quit. Her mom was a HR consultant and could work only when she had projects. It was a very stressful time for her mom as she was the only one working at that moment, and panicked about the situation. Anaya was unsure whether she'll get into a good school or not. They were even forced to change their house as their landlord required them to move out. It was the most unstable time of her life, where she had no idea about what was going to happen and her family had started considering shifting their house.

However, in a month's time everything changed. Her dad got a VP's position and her mother was offered a fellowship and many projects came into her way. Even Anaya got admission into the school that she wanted and she could feel the transition that took place in her life in just a month's time from complete uncertainty to everything getting back to normal. It was an experience that she learnt a lot from and it made her realize how anything can happen at any moment and no matter how much we plan, nothing can prepare us for what will come into our lives . I learnt a lot from what she told me and it reaffirmed my belief that nothing ever remains constant, so we should make the most of whatever situation we have.

It's a very well-known saying that time heals all wounds, and I think by far its my favorite as it is something that I have experienced and seen in other people as well. As we all need time, with time everything hurts a little less, and what hurt us earlier may not hurt us again and that's a fact of life.

CHAPTER 5

THOUGHTS

"Thoughts are the shadows of our feelings-always darker, emptier, and simpler."

-Friedrich Nietzsche

The pool of thoughts that we all keep inside, tend to simmer inside us to its own boiling point. All the accolades we have won that seemed to give us all the momentary pleasures seem to be insignificant, in times like this. If we look back, I am sure the situation is same for everyone. These so-called pleasures don't even cross our minds when faced with a situation where everything seems to be wrong.

That may be constituted just as the way of life. A time when we don't seem to be worthy to be called sum of our parts, as the parts that we do identify ourselves with join to form an entity that has much less value than what its value should be theoretically. Seemingly not important, it does haunt our dreams and thoughts more than one can ever let on.

There isn't a stop switch we can use to hinder it from programming when it surpasses its limits. No that isn't a solution to this problem, no matter how much we may want it to behave in that exact same sense. Our logic though flawed, is understandable. As which human wants to go through pain and hardship in life? We all crave that addictive head rush and all that follows and want to be in a mindless state of being happy. May it be a destination or a situation we want to experience, all it does is to take different forms but its composition never changes. And that's where we tend to find ourselves. A seemingly void cycle that possesses only us and all we do is continue in this hamster cycle that we call as life.

The causes or triggers vary from various smells, thoughts, situations, words, etc. but the end result is a predictable outcome. We welcome this pool of thoughts in such instances. At this moment, there is an intense desire to just feel greater than any other feeling we may have ever experienced. A part inside you feels disgusted at this need of yours as what has gone wrong in the wirings of your brain that makes you want to feel something that everyone else seems to run away from? Is that the way for everyone or is it just you?

But there is some hope that there are other people in this world who feel the same as you do and the desire to know you are not the only one is greater than any desire to be happy within humans. The people who we are today are so because we want to belong. Not belonging in a deep psychological sense, but something more rudimentary, more simplistic, where all we want to know that we are not alone. This support isn't to know that we will have people to fight alongside us, it is this thought that it isn't only me and that is the common link that bonds us all, no matter how different we may think we are.

THE BLUES NO ONE KNOWS ABOUT

There is this feeling of hitting rock bottom. Not in the sense of reaching place that we can't come out of, but something more like a theoretical rock bottom, something about the place that you have reached with your emotions reaching an all-time low from where you just don't know where to go.

There is this heaviness in your heart that just won't go and you know you want to release some of the pressure that has been put on you by just letting it all out, but something just stops you. It may as well be a vicious cycle that you have become a part of because you remember crystal clear all the thoughts that invaded into your head earlier and it comes again and again. It sounds like a broken record, and all you need is for it to stop.

You know that this is only temporary and you will get better, at least you think you do, but at this very moment that doesn't seem to be the case. This seems like the end, even though you never truly got a chance to actually begin. There is this feeling of loneliness that seeps through you deep within your bones, when you realize that there isn't a single person that comes in your head who you can tell what you're feeling. You won't deny the fact that people did care, but in the end when it came down to it, they just didn't care enough and that is where all your inhibitions just comes true. You always know people who aren't there for you at the end, so why does it hurt? Why is there this hollowness in your heart when the result is something that you had expected all along?

The answer is that there was always this big part of you that hoped that at the end, when it came down to it, people would be there. They would look past the fake layer that you are putting for the rest of the world and call you out. This just comes down to wishful thinking, as nothing of that sort is what actually happens in your life. The reality is that you continue to stay as a bystander in the world whereas others continue to go on doing what they always do, and the silent hints that you leave just seem to go unnoticed and so do you.

You remember sitting alone on the bridge of tears, reaching a point from where this newfound loneliness comes over but everyone around you continues to do what they have always done. With them having no idea that all you wanted was them to take the first step to realize that you're not okay.

You remember all the times when you stood your ground to be there for the people who needed you, even when there was no cry for help from their side. There was , just your silent reflection and realization that they needed you and you would be there for them. There hasn't come a time where you regret ever being there for them, but there is a part deepinside, that you thought was never there that feels the impact of the hurtful force at realizing that maybe you just don't mean to them as much as you thought you did. Something always seems to fall short and maybe it is your exceedingly high expectations, but is it too much to ask for a shoulder to cry upon without there being any call from your side? Maybe it is because it just feels like something that you have always wanted but never got to experience.

You know the way this is going to roll out like the back of your hand. You are going to feel the worst you have ever felt until it continues to a point that every little incident that had the power to make you sad swarms into your head with lightning speed, until all that is left is you and your thoughts with nowhere else to go, and no one else to go to either. You know that right after you have reached your darkest point you will see the light and return to being how you were.

Slowly the power and happiness will grow to an extent where any of your insecurities don't matter and it seems as if you have overcome them all. But all that follows is you tumbling down from the top of the hill, reaching the same exact point from where you arose with the exact thoughts plaguing your head. Again, you will awaken like a phoenix from the ashes by yourself, without the help of any external agency with the same realization, but in a new light dawning upon you.

You know this procedure like the back of your hand and all you feel is that this isn't how you want to go on living. The act of continuing to cry and obsess over the same time and again isn't a life that you are interested in living. All you want to find is a missing piece of the equation that seems to be your life just so that there is a possibility, even if a teeny tiny one that you won't feel the same way again that there is an end to all this. And no matter what you thought, your life isn't a never-ending rat race that you have participated in.

You know there will be this different side to you when you have come out of this very dry spell, and the way you look at this outcome and everything else will have a certain amount of zest to it that will make you possess a newfound appreciation of who you are. But as well as you may know, that you will be different, You also know that you are going to return to the same place that you found yourself in and that isn't something that you want to continue.

Something that feels even worse through all of this, is that you have nowhere to go. With everyone having that one person who seems to complete them, all you can feel is that you stick out like a sore thumb among them all, and that just seems to make it even worse. There are moments where you feel better and it seems like there may actually be a time when you don't feel this way all the time, that you have reached your lowest and have started returning to how you used to be only for a minute setback to occur and for you to return to the bottom point gets worse than before.

There isn't any point in sugarcoating the way that any of us will feel when you reach our lowest point, a time when all you feel is alone with no one there by your side, you feel there is a hole where your heart used to reside, and there is this new whole definition of being alone that you experience. The sad part is that it feels like forever, a time where you feel you are always going to continue to feel this way as the concept of light at the end of the tunnel is too foreign to even consider. And no matter how much someone else will tell you that it gets better or that they understand, there isn't any ounce of you that actually believes in it.

I hope I could say that I 'cured" myself from all the demons that I faced and have turned into an individual who is positive 365 days a year with nothing holding me back. But unfortunately, that isn't the case and no matter how much we would want to deny it or try to prove it otherwise, the life that we have got a chance to live is a roller coaster that sadly has half the number of downs as it has ups and there isn't an exit route that we can just take from feeling and that is something that you just need to accept; it's okay to not be okay. And it may not seem like it but there are people out there for you, willing to be there for you, even if it doesn't feel like it.

HAPPINESS

We have reached a stage in life where happiness either acts as a goal in our head or even if it is something that is in the moment, it is all dependent on certain conditions that have been set by us. Unknowingly, we have all evolved into a materialistic society, where the only happiness that we feel is when we achieve something, get good grades, win certain competitions, beat certain people, get a good salary, etc. I'll talk about happiness in both of those accounts.

So, certain people say that when they get older, one of their goals is to be happy in life. When we set happiness as a goal in our head then we have made happiness as a fixed end point where we wish to achieve this abstract concept of happiness as we feel that we aren't exactly content with how our life is at this moment. However, happiness is as fleeting as capturing any butterfly in the field, we may feel that we have captured it in a certain second but the next thing we know is that it has escaped from our grasp and there isn't anything that can be done about it.

When we sit, and wish that when certain situations change, something within us will also change that will result in us becoming happier individuals, then we are foregoing the happiness that we may feel at any moment as according to us, what we are feeling isn't happiness, what we will feel when we escape this certain situation is happiness. What is the result of our actions then? So, in hope of achieving an emotion later in our lives , whatever happiness we feel right now is discarded in the hope of something that we may or may not reach. Maybe the situation that we face right now is bad, but what is the guarantee that if we just change the premise we will also change as individuals and become happy? Our future is unknown to us, as well as everyone around us, so what if our future is worse than our present? Are we going to spend our time feeling bad for ourselves and regret not making the best of the situation?

Even if our premise does change, and we don't feel this feeling of happiness that we have craved for so long, then the only constant that is left is us. Does that mean we are the only reason we are not happy? Most of the times, this is the reason. So, if we take everything out of our line of vision and just concentrate here and now, then we should try to think about what is it that is resisting us from becoming happy and once we have found that answer, then half of our work is done. Instead of trying to hope and pray that something comes knocking down for us, we should ourselves become the change that we wish to see.

This doesn't necessarily mean that all people sit and wait for happiness to come knocking on their door, but that doesn't mean that we all understand the meaning of it. Most people around the world derive happiness from their achievements: that range from what marks they get, what clothes they wear or the various accolades that are sitting on their shelves.

In today's world where almost every person is a genius or has an extraordinary mind, there isn't any room for people to just be normal. People feel that they can't just be mediocre, they need to be completely extraordinary at something otherwise they aren't good enough to compete in this world. Just doing something for the sake of doing anything, isn't acceptable anymore. If someone is good at sports, they need to be a state or national level player, or if they are good at academics they need to possess various accolades and etc.

However, what do the rest of the people that aren't gifted with an extraordinary mind do and can't meet the unrealistic expectations that society has set on them?

Society has been designed in such a way that we all need to keep outdoing ourselves, as well as all other people around us. The insane amount of pressure that has been on us due to the changing times isn't something that can be reasonably met by anyone. People nowadays live in this world where competitiveness has reached heights, where it can't be called healthy anymore. The unreasonable expectation that has raised from us and the environment around us has resulted in us shifting our priorities to a point where we don't know why we are doing what we are doing. Studying for school, has transformed from learning to improve your knowledge, to getting better marks than people around us.

Attributes like trust, honesty, and helpfulness seem not important in relation to how successful someone can get in their life. While being competitive or even ambitious isn't something that people should be ashamed of, we shouldn't let these things overpower what we truly want to be. There are so many stories that are heard of how people lose important relations or friendships as they have let their need of being better than everyone take over who they are as people. Moreover, as humans grow older and get more mature what makes them happy, also keeps fluctuating. Whereas, when we were younger, certain actions of people would have made us happy, now only achieving something that hasn't been achieved by anyone else is what makes us happy.

Humans are creatures with a supply of never ending greed that makes them want to achieve everything under the sun and keep wanting more and more, hoping to feel content only when they do accomplish it. However, happiness isn't something that should have conditions put on it. When we don't take it at face value instead try to dig a little deep, we will find that the more conditions we put on this feeling of happiness, more hard it will be for us to try to attain it. But when we try to remove all these restrictions and conditions that have been put by the world as well by us we will realize that the chances of us being happy with who we are, is all we need.

I've always heard people say that their parents are obsessed with the marks that their children get in various examinations; however, we are being hypocrites if we say something like this because, we as a society are materialistic in everything that we do. Just doing something for the art of experience or fun, isn't something that is appreciated anymore, like I said before we need to be exceptional in everything that we do or else we feel as if we aren't good enough. This is making us an extremely career driven and ambitious society that thinks only about being better than the next person we see. Most people say that you should be the best version of yourselves and maybe to some extent we do concentrate on that, but as times are changing, our focus is also shifting into things that apparently really matter. In my opinion, all this materialism and achievement is making us generally unhappier.

I personally have been in situations where I feel I'm not good at the things that really count in life and well what is the point of that? There's this theory that someone introduced me basically states that if someone is really smart he will be called brilliant, but if someone is a really good painter he will be called a brilliant painter. Since the time I've heard this it has been on my head and is making me see the world with a completely different perspective. Not only me but people all around usually make this distinction to decide if someone actually possesses worthwhile qualities or not. However, who are we to put limitations on us and the people around to make us feel less worthy.

While someone who is considered as a genius, who is good in academics isn't on the same level as someone who has the ability to make someone feel better. When we think about it, we will realize this isn't an issue that is only found in one person; it is a universal issue that has a very few exceptions.

When we think about the number of times we put ourselves down for thinking that we couldn't be extraordinary like the rest of the people we see and went into a cycle of despair that is one of the hardest things to get out of, and that's when we should try to change our mindset. Start thinking of the small things that we do that may bring happiness for other people or ourselves.. Things so minute that we may ignore but when we try to sit and recollect about these small things in life, that is where our true happiness lies. This shouldn't be confused with us not wanting to achieve something in life or not wanting to be something.

The way that we are programmed is that we can't just stay in a state of static, we need to keep improving things and ourselves. However, when we do try to achieve different things in life, we shouldn't confuse it with us wanting to achieve happiness. As no matter how much we may want it, happiness isn't something that can be achieved. It is a state of mind that comes and goes, but if we try to get the hang of how exactly we can make happiness an independent variable, we will be happier than we ever thought was possible and isn't that what our aim has been, for as long as we can remember?

When we stop chasing happiness in everything that we do, ranging from thinking of it as a fixed goal or trying to achieve something, and instead just try to live life the way that we have always wanted to and be the type of person that we have always wanted to then we will find this happiness coming and knocking at our door, demanding us to be let in and then we can actually be the true judges of what it feels like to be happy and extraordinary.

DEPRESSION

Nowadays it has become a sort of trend for people to say that they are "depressed" when they are feeling sad. It happens so instinctively that they don't even realize when to use it, but when we use this word do we know what it actually entails? What all a person goes through when they are actually depressed. It is neither exactly a feeling that can be just awaken from nor is it a feeling that anyone would want to experience. So, before using this word to describe what we're feeling let's try to think what a person who is actually going through something as grave as this would feel.

There is a stigma around the world with words like depression, counselling, and many more. Lots of people look at this as a chance to make fun of people or even undermine them. But something that I don't understand is why do we behave like this? Whereas we don't judge someone that has been medically diagnosed with a disease like cancer, why don't people suffering from depression get the same free pass? Don't they too, require support from friends and family when going through this?

Depression has been defined as a disease, when you undergo a prolonged period of sadness, in which doing simple little acts becomes a hard process. There are various symptoms that are looked at, before someone is clinically diagnosed with this disease. A fact people don't get is that just because the scars the person receives isn't anything that can't be seen by someone doesn't mean what that person is feeling is irrelevant. People undergo a lot of problems that we know nothing about, and chances are we are never going to get to know what actually happens in someone's life, so the reasons a person gets clinically depressed may not be known to us, but that doesn't mean we can't do something to help said person.

How many people would you know that actually have the courage to face the world and state what they went through, and don't feel ashamed by it? It is very rare. There is a constant pressure that they are dealing with and whether or not they should share this detail with someone in their lives . The thoughts revolving in their head vary as , what if this spreads or what if people make fun of me or what if people don't understand me?

People that do go through this have enough on their plate, without us adding to their demise by judging them. What they really need is someone to support them through this difficult time in their lives. While we may or may not know why a person is going through this state where they really have lost all motivation in life and feel like there is no point in this life that they are living, we should do our best to help them. While some people may have suffered a tragic accident, or a really terrible incident may have happened, in some cases it is minor things happening in a child's life that accumulate to a point where they don't know how to continue from there anymore.

For example, if a child always feels that they have been neglected by their family members or friends, after a point when they are going through their hormonal changes they might reach a place after which these small feelings that they've been trying to ignore for as long as they remember can't be kept inside anymore and instead end up blowing up in their face. After they have reached their breaking point, every small action ends up opening the Pandora's box that they have kept hidden inside. Dealing with life becomes something that they have no idea how to do, and start feeling as if there is no point in them being alive.

These thoughts that a child goes through isn't something that they can just share to the outside world so they end up hiding themselves from the rest of the world and start pulling away from the rest of their friends. Activities that could get them to smile at any instant of time just don't hold the appeal that they used to. They slowly start losing interest in the little things in life and don't know how to continue them anymore.

How does one continue from a spot where their entire existence has been thrown into a system of turmoil and the question of who they are and what exactly they are doing in this life are questions they have no answer to.

So, when people judge others for being "this way," something these people need to realize is that no one wants to feel this way. If there was an off switch to the feelings that they are experiencing they would have shut it off as soon as they could. However, no matter how much we wish, sometimes our brain work the way it doesn't. We are living creatures programmed to deal with the emotions that we have as that is what separates from animals or other creatures found on this earth. Something we all need to learn is that if we can't help someone at the time of their need, we shouldn't do anything to add to their grief. We may never come to know about the problems that the person has gone through that may result in the person not being able to do everyday tasks that may seem normal for us. are It is really necessary for people all around the world to know that if someone who is going through depression or if they start to notice signs of the person slowly drifting apart from people or things that they used to like in general we should try talking to them about what is actually going on. Chances are the person wouldn't say anything but just knowing that they are important enough for people to realize that they are not being who they usually are will go a long way in making their situation a little better.

Even after asking this isn't something that we can just leave after that. This is a long process and if the person means even just a bit to us then we should try to help them as much as we can. Try to be more conscious to the things that you tell them as you don't want them to over think something that you meant no harm by: after all we don't know what goes on in a person's head. If the person seems to be in a place that they seem to not get out of, try to talk to their parents and get their perspectives on it. Ask questions regarding how he/she is behaving at home. Try to convince the parents to talk to the child about maybe seeing a counsellor; if they feel that helps.

I feel a lot of times teenagers especially feel the need to talk to someone like a counsellor but don't exactly have the courage to face their parents with this as they are too scared of what might happen. "What if they don't understand why I need help or what if they blame me for not being normal?" These are only some of the thoughts that run around our head when faced with decision. Thus, if parents themselves come to their children with this solution it will help in many ways.

Another stigma that is found all around is that if someone is going to a counsellor there is something wrong with them. A fact that needs to change in our society is that there doesn't have to be something wrong with a person for them to require help. In my opinion, people all around should go for counselling at least once in their life as we all have things in our lives about which we can't discuss with someone and there is this level of comfort at talking to someone who is a complete stranger to you that makes talking about your feelings to them easier than it would be to talk to someone who is a constant part of your life. Even if someone is going to a counsellor if they require help, there isn't anything that they should be ashamed of as the fact that they were able to gain the courage to admit that they require help, requires strength that we can't even begin to understand.

Apart from people who are clinically depressed there are many people who feel that they are going through something that is along the lines of depression that doesn't necessarily mean that it isn't something real, but in those cases, they can try to start talking to people about what they feel try to get other outlets to express what exactly they are going through. A problem in our world is that we don't know much about this and something that is outside our area of knowledge, makes us approach it very apprehensively. We need to develop awareness among people all around so that they may have certain amount of knowledge regarding how to help people in this situation. It may also result to develop certain skill sets in us, that are required for the person to deal with their emotions effectively.

What people really need in these situations is the undying support and love from their friends and family that makes them believe that no matter how bad situations get into, they will always have someone to fall back on, and that they are here to stay for them as long as they require them to.

Changes as radical as this can't exactly happen in a heartbeat, but unless steps are taken by people to change the current situation that they are facing we will never be able to get out of this slump. Once we start changing our own thought process then maybe we won't look at this word with this "taboo" as it is in the current situation.

Another aspect we all need to know about is that the person who is going through this will require people around them to have patience as this isn't some overnight activity that will change in a heartbeat, instead it is a very small drawn out process that may end with the person being just a shell of who they used to be. Even after the person ends up being able to battle this disease, they will end up being completely different individuals than how they used to be. A lot of support will be required from a person's surrounding to help them decide as to how to continue existing as a different version of themselves than how they used to be. This is a part of their life that is going to be as hard as the situation they faced earlier. A period of transition doesn't come as easily as one might think. The support they require from other people may in some ways end up in getting absorbed by them, and chances are that they may start actually believing in themselves.

Something that people in general don't need, especially not when they are in a bad place is to feel as if they are embarrassing the other person by going through something that other people aren't. No one should let anything externally or internally make them ashamed of themselves. Even though we all want to achieve this normal that everyone seems to want to achieve, in the end when we think about it who is normal in this world? Everyone has been designed in such a way to make them different from others. So, when everyone in the world is different, how do we know what are the guidelines to be normal are? Needing to let go of this normalcy is something that we all struggle with as while we all wish to be normal, we ourselves have this intense desire to be unique from the rest of the world.

The only way to solve this problem is by letting go of whatever we think we should be and instead just go on with life, doing whatever it is that we wish to achieve, leaving all preconceived notions behind. Someone always tells me, "don't think, just do," and it makes sense but when I sit and actually think about it I realize how I really need to go by that principle. As we may not realize it but the limitations that we have set for ourselves is only due to whatever we think we can do, and we never give ourselves the chance to actually decide truly what our potential is.

So, while this transition may be the hardest thing we have to go through, something that will actually make living life as well as doing something that we are actually capable of is letting go of everything: of who we think we are, or who we want to be, or what other people want us to be. All we should focus on, is building ourselves back from the ruins that we have faced and keep moving, never looking back or thinking of the "ifs and buts," just moving forward however we can and have no care for the path that we take. As long as we know what we're doing is good for us and we aren't harming anyone purposely, the destination should never matter. We may not realize it but it gets harder to move on when we have an idea stuck inside our head and when we start acting on things that contradict this idea that we have in our heads, is when we don't know how to move from the rut that we find ourselves in.

In the end, no matter what we have gone through, we should always be grateful for what we've faced as the lessons we learn by actually going through the problem teaches us something that we can't just pick up from a book or some sayings by a person. We all are the products of our decisions and at the end, it all comes down to the decisions we make and how we decide to deal with a situation that actually defines who we are as people, and what our character may be. It is very easy to feel defeated when faced with obstacles or when we feel things aren't going our way; however, it is up to us how we let anything define who we are going to be and as long as we decide to wake up every day and get ready to face whatever is thrown into our way, we will be fine and that is all we need to know.

CHAPTER 6

CHOOSE YOURSELF

"You are braver than you believe, smarter than you seem, and stronger than you think."

-Winnie The Pooh

Self-worth. These nine letters that have been strung together to form a word that holds maybe all the importance in a person's life. If there was an indicator that could measure the magnitude of self-worth found in people, more often it would be found in negative. But why has it become the norm for people around? The fact that people don't believe in themselves and feel that they're not good enough has become as common as hearing about the weather. Sometimes knowing that a person believes in himself/herself or has a good amount of self-worth or self-confidence, is as rare as the blue moon?

Is this the type of world that we want to continue to live in? Where every other person has a long list of insecurities that don't seem to end and appear to root from the fact that all they feel is that they aren't good enough. But who is that we aren't good enough for? The people who are similar to us have the same feeling or maybe people that make us feel that way.

They may simply tell us at point blank that they feel we are disappointing them and we aren't good enough to be associated with them or maybe they are subtler in their approach. But both leave us with the same feeling of insecurity.

If people, just like us feel the same way, then how is it that we feel not good enough for them, when they themselves are feeling the same. All we are achieving through this is being caught in a chase where both are attacking each other but both feel as if they are being attacked. In this world, the majority of people are dealing with insecurities that we don't know about. We all always feel that we are alone and everyone else is living a good fulfilled life, whereas we are just wasting it. However, everyone is going through insecurities whether we are aware of it or not. Then if both sides feel that they aren't good enough for the latter then doesn't that mean there is something wrong with our thinking?

On the other hand, people who put us down for their enjoyment or in order to slay their own demons, what is it that has made every word coming out of them the gospel truth? The reasons as to why they are acting the way they are won't be known to us, and that isn't our destiny to know about it. However, there is no rule that has been established, that forces us to listen to whatever it is those people think about us, as the universal truth. So, while it is easy to get into the vicious cycle of never believing in oneself because people said so, that isn't the path we should ever take. That may seem, like the easiest or even the inevitable option, but in no circumstances, shall we let people have that power over us to define how exactly good or capable we are.

The act of associating with people who play the role of degrading us, whatever chance we get is wrong on our behalf

. Distance yourself from them, and instead spend time with people who make you feel good about yourself. Then isn't it easier to listen and believe whatever they are saying about us? However, in the end no matter how much people tell us about our goodness, there is no way for us to actually believe in it until we actually believe in that too. We believing in ourselves, is the only important ingredient that we can ever come across. Like everything else, people may come along for the ride but that doesn't mean it was their journey to begin with.

Sometimes people put forward a facade of self confidence in the beginning and maybe as time progresses, they can feel the facade and become who they are in actual, by learning this art of believing in themselves... The mere act of believing in oneself, can get anyone wherever they want to go. If you don't believe in yourself, how can you expect others to do the same? However, if we do end up showing that self-belief is what we all are capable of, then there isn't any obstacle that can't be faced and broken down by us.

This is a concept as old as time, and the problems associated with it have been there since the beginning. However, there is no hero or villain in this particular story. The only obstacle that each one faces and tries to surpass is with their will and strength. So, if there are no main characters who participate in the wrong doing, then the only person at fault in the end is us. No one forced us to not believe in ourselves. No matter what they may have done, in the end it was our choice to not believe in ourselves and instead we let other external forces define something that should come from within.

There are no lessons that can be taught from this, just the realization that is needed by all of us to understand our true potential and keep working on us to get better: not as a project more, as an act of just wanting to do better for oneself. Isn't that how life is supposed to function, too?

BEING SELFISH

As we learn our true worth, there is another significant notion that we need to learn. We need to know that we need to choose ourselves and in just certain situations we should master the art of being selfish.

We may try to deny it at every turn of our existence but there are problems that we all face. It hits us at moments where we feel we can't be there for other people, or the choice comes between choosing us or them. But when it does hit us, the feeling of guilt and disappointment runs within us. It is in these times, that we feel like the worst people in the world. Varying for people across the globe, the cause for the situation is same throughout: it occurs when our ideals don't match with our actions.

As we have been growing up, there is this ideal image that we have of ourselves. We may still not think we are good enough, but there are some aspects of our lives that we are proud of us, for being that way - the one thing that sets us apart by our standards, and not by any other convention in the world. It is this ideal, that takes place in our head in such a manner that any action that points to another direction regarding these ideals, paints us in a "bad light" in our own eyes. The person that we may have inflicted this upon, may not even give it a second glance or maybe they do. But at the end, that isn't what gives us peace. The only thing that consumes us is guilt,that seems to just keep adding to our never-ending mistakes and may just tear us apart at the end.

There is this internal battle that goes on within us, where we have no idea who or what to choose: shall we choose ourselves to give us the peace of mind or the other party that may actually need us to console. Either choice is something that we can't seem to live with. If we choose the former, we are letting down this very own image of ours, right in front of our eyes and if we choose the latter, there is this breaking point, that we feel we are reaching, where we just seem to not be able to do this anymore.

Throughout this journey, there is a point where we can actually feel ourselves tearing apart and there isn't any possible solution to this impossible problem. It may feel basic,, but to go through it is something that we don't know how to overcome. In these moments, there is an intense desire within us to just let it all out, to have a listening ear for all our problems who'll understand what exactly it is that we are going through. There is this reservation about the people not understanding what it exactly is that we are going through and instead of helping us through this, they judge us. However, that is a chance that we get ready to take because this isn't something that we can do on our own, no matter how much we wish we could. This is the point where the title - life is unfair comes to the picture and all we can do is live through this unfair life which we have got a chance to live.

Our insides scream at us, no matter what the decision is and it is at this point, where we realize we need to make a decision and stick to it, as just sticking in between and doing half of both sides isn't something that is working at the least. There is a solution that is as obvious as the day to us and something that we know is what we actually want to do, but the only reason that we haven't chosen it is for the fact that it doesn't reside within our ideals. But finally, having the courage to at least say those words we decide to choose ourselves. It may make us the worst person at the end, but sometimes there is a need for us to choose us, before anyone else. It is hard when something that isn't even on the same path as what we have been doing for our whole life, but when faced with this improbable dilemma, all we can do is choose ourselves.

No matter how much we may feel like it, it doesn't make us the worst person but it is what makes us human. As no matter, how much we may want to choose someone else to be at par with our ideals, that isn't something that we can just do anymore and that is exactly something that we learn. As we grow up, this isn't taught to us but is something that we understand as we find our identity, and without this very important ideal there isn't any way that we can make it in the big bad world that everyone says we are going to live in.

There is a chance of this being taken as how to be selfish and never choose others. However, it actually means something completely different. The true implications of these words are that we should choose others, every chance that we encounter to let them know that they have us but to know that there is a limit that is sometimes reached. A limit wherein we can't continue to discard ourselves while helping others around us, as at the end there may not be any of us left to help.

ACCEPTANCE

Acceptance is something that we all struggle with, be it accepting a situation that we have been given or accepting who we are as people and trying to move on from that. I've personally struggled the most with this concept: waging a war in my head against who I should be and whom t I want to be. Then while trying to find the balance between the both, which should be who I actually am and who I' am at the end. I've struggled throughout my life to find this balance and at the end seemed to have lost this internal battle, that I had started with myself for the reasons I am still unclear about.

It may seem simple in theory. Accept the situation or the person that you are and then move on from there, but what if I am not someone who can accept what I've been given.. All I was involved in was the act of wishful thinking, hoping and praying for whatever was going on to just stop and instead transform into what I wanted to be. But that is not the way how life works, right? We all must have learnt that by now. If there is something that we want to change, it isn't going to happen by sitting and waiting around for mystical forces to change everything. Sometimes, we do want the easy way out, to just get out of what we are facing and if we just get help from another outside force then that just makes everything even easier.

However, while we may have people in our lives to be there for us, no matter what we're facing, there is a limit to which they can help us. After a point, all that can be done is by us. People can only participate in helping us by giving us the moral support. And like it's said, we came into this life alone, we will leave it alone. People are going to be there for the process, but at the end, it is what we do to fight against what we are facing and that will define how we can best learn and get better from any particular situation.

There was a point in my life, where all I could feel is disappointment for being the type of person that I had grown to be and was more than unhappy with how my life was. I remember all the days that went by with me just hoping and praying for something to change, how my life was at that time, for me to just not be who I was and things to just change. Even though I wanted this with all my heart there wasn't anything that I was ready to actually do to change this so called worst moment of my life. Wishful thinking was all my life had come down to in no way were any steps taken by me to maybe change this dream of mine into a reality, wondering that if you really want, won't there be some way in which the universe will help you to turn it into a reality? Despite my very "fool proof" plan there weren't any advancements I found in this aspect. Days and days went by, and all I could feel was disappointment, disappointed at the fact that life didn't have any favors to grant me at this one little thing that I had asked for! Is life supposed to function like this? Is this the bleak future that I am subjecting myself to? What is the point of all of this? These were some of the thoughts that roamed in my head time and again.

It all seems blur now, but sometimes when I look back, at how I used to be and what my life used to be like, I can remember it all like watching my life in a flashback. Slowly from that point, as I started growing and facing life like I used to be there were so many things that I learnt from this. May be I was just being dumb and unrealistic about life, but what I have learnt is that I need to accept who I am, who I used to be and what type of a person that I am going to become. There is no moving on, without accepting who I am. That is the most important ingredient of moving on, and all I was doing by fabricating a make-believe idea in my head was not accepting who I am. The only thing that I got, out of trying to live a life l filled with disappointment and dread. Now, when I have finally accepted my life like it is and am actively trying to change the situations that I don't like or the attributes that I personally wouldn't want to continue having in myself, is a life filled with much more content than the one I was used to living.

We as humans, don't want to continue living a life where we feel stuck and would like anything to get us out of it and as fast as that can happen. As much as we would like to be there , there isn't any formula or method that we can adopt to fasten this process. All we can do is try to go through whatever it is and at the end when we have reached a good place, that is when we will either involuntarily or voluntarily start taking steps towards the direction we want to.

This is like anything else in life, when there is any situation that makes us unhappy, angry or upset, there is no point in trying to deny those feelings and push it into a deep corner of our head. All that it achieves is those feelings to prolong for much longer than necessary. Denial may be the first step to recovery but that doesn't mean that we continue to be stuck there.

Acceptance may be the most important thing that we can learn and it is something that we all should know how to do. No matter what it is, if we want to pave the process to recovery, the only way to go about it, is by accepting everything and this is something that should be stressed time and again by people all around us. And there was this thing that my friend told me. She said the more you hear people around you telling something can be done, more are the chances of you to actually believe in it.

After we do accept ourselves, there is this complete serenity that we get to experience if we are true to ourselves by making sure everyone knows who we are. The act of being an ideal version of ourselves seems to achieve only one feat and that is making us go far from who we truly are and hide our true selves, making us live a kind of double life. This is the reason most of us don't know what to say when we're asked who we are, as we have been lying to ourselves and others for so long that such an easy question becomes something to which we don't have an answer.

There is a power that resides in knowing who you are and accepting it that gives us a feeling of complete peace where we know who we are and we are proud of it. If we only are ashamed of who we are, then how can we expect others to accept us? As we continue in this path, there is something that we feel shifting within us and all we will know for sure is that we are happy being who we are and there isn't anyone we'd rather be, not now, not today and not ever. As one's individuality is a gift, that has been given to us and it would be shame on us if we let it go waste due to our misconceptions.

So, when you finish reading this, I want you all to ask yourselves who you are and whatever may be the first thing that pops into your head, accept it, and keep the walls open for all the various thoughts that rise within you for the question and just simply accept it all. To know who you are is one of the best gifts that we can ever receive and also one of the easiest feats to accomplish.

BLURBS

"A relatable and eye-opening take on the recurring melancholy of a teenager's life. Aanandi Sidharth has captured the savory that everyone tastes through their formative years."

- Aditya D Menon

"This book is based on a teenager's life and the most unique part about it is the way it connects so many people. The language, stories and every small thing about Spero connects with the teenagers and that's why it's such a delight to read."
- Sakshi Chandak

"The book is a delight to read. The way Aanandi has spoken what's inside a teenager's mind is truly thought provoking."
- Neeraj Khanna

About the Author

Aanandi Sidharth

date of birth: 9th May, 2000

Aanandi has made a debut attempt with her book named Spero. She is a seventeen years old budding writer who aspires to share stories which resonate with different people. She is hardworking, kind, confident and most importantly strong. Being fueled by passion and enthusiasm, she hopes to create stories that make a difference.

The idea of writing a book had always been on her mind, but it wasn't until recently after a certain encouragement was she able to start on this process. She wanted to write this book in order to give people a feeling of belonging and for them to know that they're not alone. This was something that she felt was a huge problem with teenagers these days: with all of them feeling that what they go through makes them alone and separated from everyone else. However, they couldn't be farther from the truth. This book, also gives parents a sneak into the mind of teenager's minds of teenagers that helps to understand them more.

The process started initially when she began interviewing people of various age groups, to get what they felt about various issues and ideas these days. There are many instances that she has recorded from those individuals and has mentioned them in the book to depict real-life scenarios, people go through.

Going ahead , she wishes to continue writing and come up with more stories that wike make a difference to people and maybe, willeven help a few along the way.

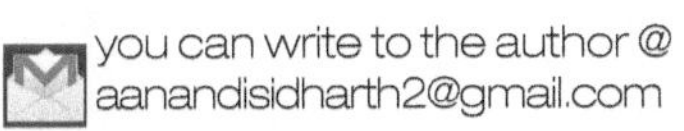

you can write to the author @
aanandisidharth2@gmail.com

follow the author

https://www.facebook.com/aanandi.sidharth.3

SPERO

Aanandi Sidharth

Did you like the book **?**

Email your
questions, experiences, and suggestions
to the author at
aanandisidharth2@gmail.com

CROWD-FUNDERS

(NAMES LISTED ALPHABETICALLY)

Aadarsh Sidharth

Aakarsh Sidharth

Aanandi Sidharth

Aarshia Chakraborty

Abishek Raman

Aditya D Menon

Aditya Desu

Aishwarya Patil

Akash Gudi

Ananya Sreewastav

Aneesh Sidharth

Anitha Raghunath

Anjum Parwez

Anshuman Gill

Anumita Vaishnavi

Aradhana Walia

Archana Chhabra

Arpita Sahu

Arvind Nayar

Arvinder Kaur

Atman Soni

Bandana Sreewastav

B N Jha

Chinmaya Punja

Devavrath H

Dr. Pawan Kumar

Garima Singh

Gayatri Visvanathan

Geetha Vishwanathan

Indu Jha

Jaideep Walia

Jayani Patil

Jeeva Annie Varghese

Jeril Jacob

Jerin John

Jitesh Sharma

Jyotsna R

Katyayni Singh

Kavita Sikka

Manu Khosla

Mihika Baitahji

Mona Malhotra

Namita Verma

Natasha Praveen

Nathan Jayaraman

Naveen Kumar

Nesha Prabahar

Nihar Mishra

Nikhil Varma

Nitya Dintakurti

Ojas Bardiya

Pallavi Kumari

Partha Dutta

Pawan Singhal

Pooja Roy

Prachi Seth

Pradeep Arya

Prateek Jha

Prithika Ramaiyer

Putul Mishra

Rahul Jha

Rajashree Ivaturu

Rajkumar Jha

Ranjini Rao

Rimmy Augustine

Rishi Chhapolia

Ritesh Tota

Rohit Kashyap

Sakshi Chandak

Saniya Sood

Sanjay Jha

Shaveta Sahni

Shefali Tyagi

Shincy Cijo

Shivani Bhamidipati

Shreshtha Menon

Shreyas Sudhir

Shweta Srivastava

Siddharth Mishra

Sudha Roy

Sumeet Jha

Sumita Jha

Surendra Jha

Sushmita Prithiani

Tanya Punjani

Tasneem Dasgupta

Usha Jha

Veena Rao

Vrinda Rao